QUICK Stories for QUICK Kids

ANN

AGES 6 plus

Stefan Nicholson

"No time to stare at funny pictures and big words. No time for getting a sore bottom from sitting down all day. No time for getting sore eyes from looking at a computer or tired hands from holding a heavy book for a long time. Read a **QUICK** story together – but read it **WELL**"

- Stefan Nicholson

Quick Stories for Quick Kids

First Edition 2019 **print book**

Envirosupport Publishers

P.O. Box 370, South Hobart,

Tasmania, Australia 7004

ISBN 978-0-6482953-9-6

Contacts:

Website: www.stefannicholson.com

Email: stefannicholson@bigpond.com

Phone: +61 417 181 077

Books: https://www.amazon.com/author/stefannicholson

Contents

Introduction 4

Xavier's Wheels 5

Back to Hobart 6

Malcolm Magpie 7

Buzzzzz 12

Little Marcus 13

Cheeky Monkey 19

My Friend 20

Isabella and the Prince 21

Roxy Dog 32

Windswept 34

Introduction

There is no TIME for an introduction . . . oh, if you insist.

Hi, my name is Stefan and I have written some **QUICK** stories just for you.

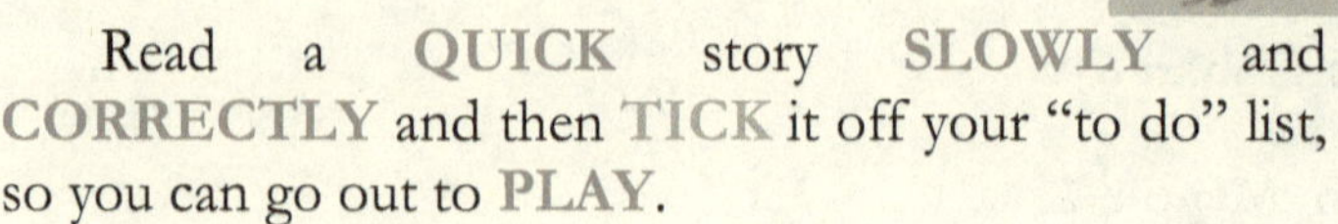

Read a **QUICK** story **SLOWLY** and **CORRECTLY** and then **TICK** it off your “to do” list, so you can go out to **PLAY**.

Got to run now . . . I can write a lot more words but it is time for me to make more friends and **PLAY** as well. Sorry, can’t stop and chat . . .

WHY?

Because when you have already spent the whole day at school and finished your homework and your Mum and Dad then want you to read something by yourself (or even better, to have them read **WITH YOU**) . . . then you need a **QUICK** story so that you can go outside to **EXERCISE** and have plenty of time to **SOCIALISE**.

QUICK . . . **QUICK** . . . you can read a **QUICK** story right **NOW** and finish it.

Don’t look at the pictures if you really want to save some more **TIME**.

Stefan Nicholson

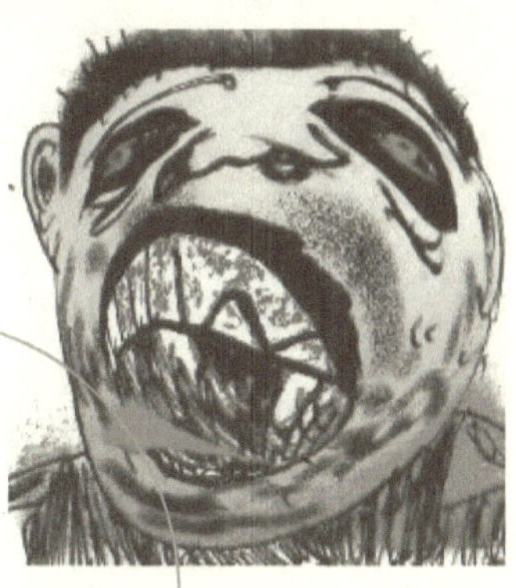

Xavier's Wheels

Zoe told me the story about a hero boy who laughs out aloud as he crashes each toy and his name is Xavier.

A little rascal having fun – it was not bad behaviour.

Now when a giant stole all the wheels (to eat with his glass and plastic meals and two fat horses and a yellow duck), taken from cars and planes and a monster truck, then the world we knew was not the same. Until Xavier hatched a plan – now this was no game!

Zoe said her brother worked hard for days on end, to make a pie that he could send to the giant's house high up in the sky. It was a round-wheel pastry potato pie.

Xavier pushed the pie through the giant letterbox, then off to the front door, where he knock, knock, knocks!

> The giant shouted angrily, "Who is there?" for to have a visitor, why it was so extremely rare.
>
> Xavier replied, "I've baked a giant pie in the shape of a wheel, and I've come to offer it to you as a special deal, for our cars and planes and trucks stand still and if you eat all our wheels, it will surely make you ill.
>
> But if you give them back, why I promise you that I'll bake another pie – maybe one, maybe two.
>
> And you must promise me now that no more will you steal. Especially each driving, steering, meant-for-moving wheel."

Back to Hobart

If you are heading back to Hobart on an autumn day, you will see the mountain rising over Sandy Bay. When you feel that light wind blowing up from old Iron Pot, then, you know you are surely blessed with you've got.

Come and roam our island home.
You will always have a place to call your own.
Hear the wind call you home.
It is time. Return with sails aloft, full blown.

Have you heard the cat play fiddle in the city mall, or have you shopped in Salamanca at a market stall. Or explored the Channel sailing out from Oyster Cove? Oh, there is always somewhere close, to rest or rove.

Come and roam, fresh air and crashing foam.
See the rolling hills and rivers flow.
Hear the wind call you home.
It is time. Return with sails aloft, full blown.

Note: This is a song.

Malcolm Magpie

A magpie sat on my TV, and started singing instantly.

So I said, "What are you doing, singing like that? You know I've fed you lean, so you won't get fat."

But Malcolm magpie – that's his name, said my excuse was rather lame. Pointing to the advert of a huge meat pie, he squawked,

"Get me one of those and away I'll fly."

Well, I got a huge meat pie from the baker, and the doctor gave me a second-hand pacemaker just in case Malcolm's arteries could not cope. Aye, that bird thinks his smart but he is really such a greedy dope.

When he saw that whopping pie he gulped it all down, then true to his word he flew off wobbling hesitantly into town. But what he was really searching for was that baker's shop, even though he could feel he was about to pop!

So, he strapped up the pacemaker to his fat, wobbly chest. No silly Malcolm – it goes under your vest! And when he dropped from the sky, from the pressure of that huge meat pie, people thought he would explode . . . and they quickly passed him by!

Ahem! That is everyone except one. Yes, of course it was me! For the outcome was as expected, I knew what it would be. That is why I followed greedy Malcolm, with a big wheel-barrow and a strong cup of tea.

As I wheeled him home, he just stared at the shops, showing cakes and pastries, and beef pies and pork chops in the windows as we passed. And he thought . . . that if he had all the money in the world, there was not one thing he would have bought.

He told me so with his weepy eyes but did not say a word. There was no time for lies for this broken bird, about why he wanted more food than he could possibly eat, that led to his fall towards my tired waiting feet.

What could I say? He was so sorry and hurt, enough to have learnt not to eat until you burst. But suddenly within me, I felt more for the poor. For it is as well he did not fall near their hungry door.

But I'm off at an angle already, away from my tale about this greedy magpie and his epic dietary fail.

For when Malcolm and I got back to my home, it was time to organise my heavy, bright-blue gnome, as it was now his job to look after this daft podgy bird, surely the most lazy, sneakiest, cunning magpie you have ever heard.

What is that you say? A gnome is just a painted stone, of course made out of cement and not likely to roam. But this gnome was different, for it once was a prince, cursed three times over, for stealing Greenie's prime lean mince.

Yes, the prince had also been greedy, as bad as Malcolm they say and he would go off in a rage if he did not get his way. So he stole the mince, meant for that green frosty witch. Oh, surely not the nice kind at all, living in that dark, smelly ditch.

The prince could not move or talk but could hear and understand, thinking that Malcolm just might be persuaded to give him a helping hand. In exchange for releasing the string, which bound them together, he would offer the witch every one of Malcolm's lovely feathers!

You see with those feathers, she could make up her favourite magic spell and in return, she would indeed free the prince from his bright blue prison cell.

So, the prince told Malcolm to sharpen his beak on his painted blue stone, knowing full well his feathers would fall out, leaving him with bare skin and bone, except for his big podgy belly which was cold . . . no doubt.

Now when the witch flew down on her yellow dry-straw broom, she saw bare Malcolm and that princely gnome amongst all the scattered feathers in the room.

She quickly gathered every feather then released the waiting prince, who could now shake off his dusty garment, like a very blue powdery rinse.

Then she crept up on poor Malcolm all shivering, wobbling and cold. With her evil spells, his plump round body could be salted-and-peppered and rolled. To be made into bread! Well, according to Malcolm, that is what she said.

But what's that you say? What do you mean with "Where were you pray, when all this was happening to the prince and Malcolm too . . . surely there was something that you could do."

Well there was . . . and I did . . . and I can tell you now that I secretly hid, for I was waiting for that witch to free the greedy prince. He had endured enough time to feel sorry for stealing the witch's mince and I would get three wishes whereas you would get only one. Then I'd be ready to run fast before the witch knew where I had gone.

I would save the prince, teach him not to steal and make Malcolm reason that whatever food he sees, is not to be eaten in between my fine healthy meals.

But of course the witch was also tricked into freeing the prince from his blue gnome casing and she started to wince! I've never seen anything more angry or horrible since.

Oh dear, I had not thought about that . . . and also, poor Malcolm had been tricked by the prince and was now featherless where he sat.

It looks like the prince had another lesson coming, which was to learn how to treat one another. A bit late it seems I know, for me to guide him like a father or a mother.

It was clear he had not learnt what is right and what is wrong, so I had to teach him with a simple trick using a familiar bird-like song.

Oh yes, the magpie's call is sweet and bright but not if it is always there, in your ears, loud and shrill. It would make you scream. Am I right? It would most certainly make you ill.

The prince, now cleaned from his concrete coat, started giving orders, ignoring Malcolm and he was beginning to gloat.

So I took his jewelled crown that had been put down and placed a speaker in there, just as he turned, shouting with a frown.

> "What are you up to . . . to give me such a scare? Put my crown down you lowly creature. It must never be touched by anyone except by me. It is a most expensive royal feature."
>
> "But, but . . . ," I tried to say but he was gloating again.

The speaker had not been found. Therefore, I left the room and counted to ten . . . before turning on full volume, that familiar magpie sound. It was loud and sharp and filled his head with shrieks. He jumped and fell, and covered his ears, but the sound from the speaker was from many angry magpie beaks.

> "Stop the noise, please stop it and I'll make things right now. Oh, never again will I treat another with spite if you'll only stop and show me how."

Malcolm raised his head and offered a warm smile.

> "I'll help you prince but it will maybe take a while to not be greedy, steal or treat others with scorn. We didn't learn to behave properly it shows, from the moment we were born."

That is the end. Yes, it really is quite plain and short . . . my tale about greedy Malcolm and how a prince and a witch got caught, all trying to deceive each other without a care or even a kindly thought. You may be wondering if they learnt to treat all living things with care. Ah, I see you thinking they did not . . . and now look to see what I wrote next . . . and stare.

Now I will not say another word, for to do so would only bring on sneers. All because you expect me to say, that they were always good, for years and years and years.

But will this change the way YOU live? . . . Will it change the way YOU feel? . . . Will YOU ever lie or maybe think about an item YOU can steal? . . . or treat your friends so horribly bad, like the prince and Malcolm and the witch? That would make me very sad.

But not you, I can tell . . . it is not your way! Oh and for the record with our story friends, I have even seen them happily play. I did, I did. I think it was in the month of May.

Now, whenever you hear a magpie sing and play . . . remember Malcolm Magpie on that day.

Buzzzzz

I know I have never Thylacine,

Unless it happened when I have jumping been.

Shhhh! Have I just now a lion snoring heard, or could it maybe be a Bee trapped in my lemon curd?

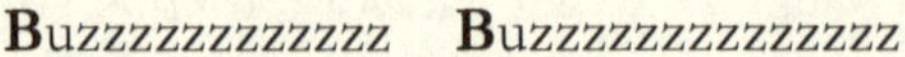

Buzzzzzzzzzzzz **B**uzzzzzzzzzzzzzz

Where's that river, now just where did Derwent?

Did it fall by mountain top descent? Amongst the clouds, with wind and rain so near

Whoa, look! I can see all around Tasmania.

Note: A Thylacine is a Tasmanian Tiger. They say that there are none left in the world . . . but I think there a quite a few. The Derwent is a river that flows through Hobart, which is the capital city of Tasmania.

Little Marcus

"What are we going to do with little Marcus?" said his father, shaking his head.

Marcus was not a happy boy at the best of times, but today he was both sad and angry because he did not like his birthday presents. He wanted a space-rocket and an electric car . . . and also a huge sailing boat so that he can wave and jeer at all the town's folk from the river, as they make their way to work and school.

Little Marcus was convinced that his parents did not love him anymore, or else they would have given him what he wanted, as usual, instead of a silly tree-house and that silly golden crown.

Yes . . . Marcus was a prince.

He ran out of the castle clutching the crown and hid in one of the old horse stables. After kicking over some buckets of water and throwing himself into a mound of hay, he was surprised to find an old oil lamp buried in the hay, next to him. He looked at it carefully and thought about the story of the Genie and the Lamp.

"Oh I wish that I could have three wishes' for my birthday, then I could get anything and everything I want," he said sadly to himself.

Well, the very next moment there was a huge 'swooshing' sound as green and purple smoke came pouring out from the spout of the lamp. It lasted a good ten seconds before coming to a stop. When the smoke had cleared, an irritated looking genie stood before him, arms crossed and sporting a most

disagreeable looking snarl. He looked as though he had been sleeping . . . for a LONG time.

"What do YOU want then? I suppose that you must have asked for a wish, or I wouldn't be standing here," bellowed the Genie with a most horrible scowl.

"I asked for three wishes actually," replied little Marcus with his hands on hips, "and I had better tell you that I am a prince . . . so there!"

You see little Marcus was a spoilt little boy who always got what he asked for – unlike today. The genie looked at him and gave a long sigh. Then looked at him again, closely to determine just what sort of a boy this was – what with his demands and apparently greedy idea of what he was entitled to ask for.

"Three wishes you say? Hmmm . . . Let's just start all over again and I want you to ask me what you want, in a more polite way, alright?" said the Genie with a very funny look on his face.

"Alright! Give me three wishes then, or else I'll . . . I'll throw your lamp into the river," replied little Marcus.

The Genie was now fully awake and could see that little Marcus needed to be taught a very good lesson.

"By the laws of Solomon Sunday Saladin Salabim, I will grant you three wishes if that is what you want. So ask me again what you wish for . . . nicely!"

Little Marcus grinned and rubbed his hands together. He thought that he would get as much out of this situation as he could – even by cheating if necessary.

"OK then, I wish you would give me three wishes . . . please," said little Marcus defiantly with gritted teeth.

"So, you WISH to have three wishes. Is that correct?" said the Genie

"Yes it is. Give me three wishes. And I want them now!" snapped little Marcus.

The genie just smiled and raised his hands in the air. He looked back down at little Marcus.

"Your wish is my command . . . now you have two wishes left."

"But . . . but that's cheating. That was not a wish. I wanted three wishes, not two."

The genie looked very snooty and pleased with himself. He lowered his head down to whisper into little Marcus's ear.

"See what happens when you try to be a clever clogs lad? I tell you what . . . how about you wish for a birthday EVERY day of the year. Imagine that! Presents and cake and ice-cream every day of the year because it is your birthday. Do you want to wish for that?"

"Oh yes, yes . . . I wish that I had a birthday every day of the year starting today! Oh, every day showered with presents. Yes, that is what I want," shouted little Marcus.

The genie just smiled again and raised his hands in the air. He looked back down at little Marcus.

"Your wish is my command. Now you have one wish left so you had better use it . . . wisely."

Little Marcus was not listening. He was planning in his head all the presents that he wanted, starting with a space-rocket and that huge sailing boat. Meanwhile, the genie had taken out his calculator and was humming away to himself, with the occasional shaking of his head.

"Oh dear . . . oh dear, I am presuming that you are only nine years old my prince, but that does not seem to help you very much at all," murmured the genie.

"What are you talking about? What are you doing? I want my last wish to tell everybody in the world that it is my birthday EVERY day," screamed little Marcus.

The genie looked at Marcus and shook his head.

"Oh, I can't see you with a long beard and grey hair at all. No . . . not with a crown as well. And then there are all those presents . . . no room left in the entire castle. And how fat you would become eating like that every day."

Little Marcus was beginning to think that the genie had gone quite mad. The genie continued murmuring.

"Good, let me see now. You are nine today . . . that means you will be ten tomorrow . . . and at the end of this month . . . oh, dear you will be thirty . . . and by Christmas day . . . you will be ninety years old."

Little Marcus was mortified. His chin dropped, his eyes looked like golf balls and his head was spinning.

"You . . . you tricked me again. You are a bad genie and I will throw your lamp into the river this instant," screamed Marcus.

The genie shook his head slowly and felt a bit sorry for poor little Marcus.

"You are never satisfied with anything and take everything for granted. You always want more and more and more of everything . . . and now you have it. More birthdays and more presents . . . and now more often . . . just as you wished."

The genie thought about the situation as Marcus began to cry.

"I have been so silly and greedy in my life and now I have ruined it all because I did not get what I wanted for my birthday. Any other boy would have been so very happy and grateful for such presents," sobbed Marcus.

The genie was beginning to think that he was being just as bad. After all, although he had been disturbed from his sleep by a greedy little boy, it was no reason to ruin his life, which was now apparently only three months longer!

"Now see here Marcus . . . I may have been a bit harsh with you but I wanted to teach you an important lesson. I presume that you want to be a king one day . . . a good king at that, who looks after his people and cares for others. Now . . . if you agree to change your ways to become a better person . . . then I may have a solution for you . . . you do have one wish left you know," said the genie.

"Oh I will, I will, I promise you that. I will be kinder and not be greedy any more . . . and I will help the town's folk with their work and their lives," cried Marcus with his fingers crossed behind his back.

"Right then, you may want to expand the interval between your birthdays to say three hundred and sixty five and one quarter days, to give yourself a longer life. Of course, that means the end of your wishes . . . if you wish for that," said the genie calmly.

Marcus thought about the lesson he had learnt and was smart enough to know that his greed was the tool that the genie had used to fool him.

"Yes, I wish that each of my birthdays are three hundred and sixty five and one quarter days apart."

The genie smiled once again and raised his hands in the air. He looked back down at little Marcus who was much relieved.

"Your wish is my command. Now you have no more wishes . . . but you have used the last wish wisely," said the genie.

Marcus looked at the genie and smiled back.

"I have ended up where I started haven't I?" asked Marcus.

The genie placed the golden crown onto little Marcus's head.

"No Marcus . . . you have started off how you will end your days."

In the background, the king was looking at the situation closely and he was very happy, for it was he, who had placed the lamp in the hay and had hired an actor to play the part of a genie.

In fact, the genie had not actually DONE anything except teach little Marcus a very important lesson.

Cheeky Monkey

You will never ever catch me
As I jump and swing around.
On your table, 'cross the lounge room,
Through the air – then gone to ground.

I am yellow like a 'nana',
With a wit to test your nerves.
But you'll never ever catch me
With my twists and turns and swerves.

I will tease you, never leave you
And if you try to pin me down.
Then I will play up like I am at the zoo
To make you squirm and frown.

My Friend

My friend has a pet that he won as a bet. Sort of roundly square, with tufts of rough blue hair.

It has no bottom. It has no top. All I can see is a middle and that I believe is the lot.

He calls it "Spit" but it does not know its name
Which is just as well I am told in haste,
'cos it looks from both ends, just the same.

It keeps one eye on its food in the big red shiny bowl
But I always put it back on its face in the hole.
The other eye just stares at the stars in night's sky.
I swear that this is true, but I am more prone to lie.

It is true that my friend has a pet.
Part bird, part giraffe and flies a private jet
You must all believe that I could not possibly conceive
In my wildest dreams, such a creature
That is calm and cute and soft . . . but sometimes may also
Eat You.

Isabella and the Prince

There is a tiny kingdom called Hermania situated high up in the snow-capped mountains, like a lonely nest perched up high in a poplar tree. It is said to have a population of around two thousand people.

It snows all year round and is surrounded by dense forests with thick cotton-wool shaped clouds lower down the mountain. This is the reason that no one has have ever been there. Some people think that it does not exist at all . . . but then they would be wrong, for I have seen it briefly myself.

It was ten years ago today that I became very sick after being swept away by an avalanche into deep snow. I fell into a long sleep. When I awoke briefly, I was in a forest house in Hermania. This story is about what I believe to be true, for all I know is that when I awoke the next time, I was surrounded by my own people. They were all amazed that I was completely healthy and cured of my injuries.

What I am going to tell you is what a Princess told me as I was recovering . . . although my parents say that I had only been dreaming. But how I was cured of my sickness and injuries, in a lost two weeks in the cold snow and howling mountain winds is a mystery.

In Hermania, people are born and people die without knowing any other kind of life. Life is fun there. They do not know any different ways of living. There is no law and so no police. There is no money and so no shops or banks . . . and no schools.

The older men and women often sit in front of their big open fire-places, dreaming about their younger days when they played in the forests before returning home to a big family dinner. They admire their sons and daughters and how they have grown into adults . . . just like themselves.

The people do not work in factories or offices but merely live well and look after each other like a huge family. There is no need for laws because everyone is friendly and help each other without being asked. They do not kill or steal or fight one another because all are equal. What possessions they have are passed down to their sons and daughters or given to their neighbours and friends.

They do not know what money is for, because if anyone wants butter, bread or fruit or water to drink, then they repay their neighbours with something of equal value. If they have a good harvest, they would likely give away their produce or store it for the future.

Because there are no schools, the people are ignorant of the outside world and indeed, do not think that other lands exist outside of Hermania. I do not know what they ever thought of me!

The children are taught to obey their parents, help with jobs and to sew, knit and bake . . . or help to build new houses. Each one chooses to learn a special skill well that suits their own liking and personality. They are happy to be themselves.

They cannot read or write and so they are unable to find out about their ancestors or the natural world around them, except for the information told to them by their parents. The only information they know is for everyday living.

As it is always cold, each family will make sure that big log fires are always burning inside their houses. The children, with their red-cheeked faces sprinkled here and there with flakes of snow, gather up wood for the fire and put pinecones on the fire to give the air a sweet smell.

The parents take turns in looking after the crops and vegetables, as well as the animals, which sleep in barns hidden in the forests, by the sides of the mountains. The barns are warm and the animals are well fed and very comfortable.

The entire family share the household chores, becoming their own bakers, tailors and cleaners. Safety, health and welfare are critical parts of protecting the family from those things that make us sick and injured. They all have a sense of pride in their appearance and way of life. They want for nothing.

They do not know that the rest of the world would consider them primitive . . . if they ever met anyone.

I said at the start that Hermania is a kingdom and so it is . . . with a King, a Queen and their daughter the princess Isabella.

Now I did say that everyone is equal in this place and I still stick to that idea in theory . . . even though the above mentioned family live in a castle. No ordinary castle either, for it is magnificently carved out of the beautiful shiny blue rock found on only one part of the entire mountain. One side has a very steep cliff, which appears bottomless because of the clouds at the bottom. On the other sides are the houses of the loyal subjects.

Nobody knew why they had to have a Royal Family but they all like the idea and think that it is just another job – a job that they don't want to do. After all, the Royals have to endure the cold castle on their own, while planning and organising important events, apart from dressing up in some silly clothes and wearing spiky rings on their heads. The other thing that is unusual is that the Royal Family can read. Not that the villagers resent that because they think that reading is not necessary . . . and in fact think it is a waste of time.

The King wakes at 5 o'clock every morning and changes into his Royal organising clothes before putting on his crown. Because nothing important actually happens in Hermania, he spends most of the day flying his kite.

The Queen's job is to train the Princess into becoming a Queen but as this is not a very busy job, the Queen and the Princess are often seen climbing up the walls of the castle in their own Royal clothes and crowns . . . untangling the King's kites.

The town's people are again very happy that they are not subjected to such a dangerous lifestyle.

You might be thinking that all would be peaceful in Hermania and they all lived happily every day, forever. But hear my story out!

For in the outside world, a war was going on, as per usual and one of the nastiest witches of all, Grusella, who thankfully hated snow, became involved in the latest war by placing a spell on the Prince of the Sand People who lived near the sea.

Now this was no ordinary spell, for it made the Prince turn bright purple with horrible bumpy red spots. His own people were shocked at his appearance and feared they too would catch some disease from him. So after he had fallen asleep, they left him in the forest at the bottom of the mountain, just underneath the clouds. By chance, it was the same mountain that Hermania was located.

They left him some food, something to drink and a book to read . . . funnily enough it was called: "The Mythical Kingdom of Hermania".

Oh and there was a message 'DO NOT COME BACK – EVER' pinned to his hat, that he could not see at first because he was wearing it. He started to feel very hungry and decided to eat a little of the food. He enjoyed it so much that he soon found that there was nothing left.

When he realised that he had been dumped in the wild with no way of getting home and now with no food, he started to feel very sad. This only lasted about ten minutes however, because he was hit on the head by a very large object.

It was a kite and it had knocked off his hat and thrown him to the ground. It was then that he read the note on his hat.

An interesting thing suddenly came to mind. The markings on the kite seemed to match the very same markings on the cover of his book. Just as he was working this out, he realised that the kite was moving along the floor and then working its way up the jagged edges of the mountain. Someone was pulling the string!

He grabbed his belongings and followed the kite . . . up the cold mountain track covered in snow, first in and then out of the fluffy white clouds, until he emerged into a forest overlooking a small field. It was full of sheep, cows, goats and chickens. There was also a dam and a few sheds for the animals.

The kite disappeared up a steep cliff towards what looked like a shiny blue castle. He decided to hide out with the sheep in their shed because the weather was cold and snowy, as expected high up in the mountains. Looking down, he could see the fluffy clouds floating like someone had poured milk into a large bowl of porridge.

After a few days, the Prince became very hungry and cold and he was forced to steal milk from the cows and eggs from the noisy hens. This alerted the farmers to ask anyone if they had been on their farm and borrowed some of their supplies. No one had.

This went on for about two months until a group of villagers coming home from work on their farms saw the shadow of a purple looking 'beast' roaming the forest. Of course they exaggerated and said it was ten feet high.

As this was an unknown threat to their lives and their families, they organised a whole day in which all the villagers would search the forest for this menace to their safety. Meanwhile in the castle, King Herman (oh, yes they are all called Herman by the way) and Queen Kate were worried for their daughter's safety, as Princess Isabella had decided to walk alone in the forests that same day. She was very nosy but also very brave and this was not the first time that she had been there . . . usually to rescue the King's kite after it had blown down the mountain.

After the villagers had gone home and found nothing and convincing themselves that what they had seen was just shadows, Isabella decided to check out the area for herself. After all, she did not know danger at all and she was wearing her warmest clothing and crown.

Now it so happened that the Prince was hiding inside an old tree near the mountain path which enters into 'forbidden territory'. It was the same path that the kite had taken, as it was being pulled up by Isabella herself a few months before.

Isabella soon became tired and decided to take a nap amongst the forest flowers, right beside the tree where the Prince was hiding.

He stared at this girl with the tell-tale crown, realising that as she looked so nice and calm that maybe she would help him . . . and that incredibly, she was a Princess. But then he turned away and hid his face, knowing that the Princess would be afraid of his appearance.

There was one chance that he could speak with her. The horrible spell that was cast on him by Grusella had one weak point. Every full moon for only six hours after midnight, the Prince would return to normal. He quickly scribbled a note to leave by her side and made his way back inside the tree, scrambling through the tight entrance and knocking the book he was carrying in his backpack onto the floor.

The noise woke up the Princess and she was surprised that two hours had passed and she was late for dinner. Glancing in surprise, first at the note and then at the book on the floor nearby, she hurriedly gathered them up with the rest of her belongings and ran back to the bottom of the cliff where a hoist was ready to winch her back up to the castle.

She read the note and flicked through the book which had funny pictures of what the Sand People thought about Hermania . . . and if it even existed. Her wide-eyed expression changed into a smile and a bit of a laugh at what was written in the book. These were the same false stories that she had told "someone" else many years before.

The note said that the Prince wanted to meet her alone and not to tell anyone. So being brave and honest, she kept a promise to herself to meet him alone, to see if she could help him. She also decided to leave food and drink for him every day, next to the tree where he was hiding.

The full moon came in one week and the Princess waited by the tree at midnight. The Prince was watching her and noticed his skin changing back from being purple with red spots to just being his normal self.

He slowly emerged from the tree and for a moment, they both stared at each other. Sometimes it is possible to like another person just by looking at them and seeing if they smile. Then, there is the awareness of their soul from looking into their eyes.

They talked for a while, with the Prince telling Isabella about the curse put on him by Grusella, as well as what it is like in the land of the Sand People. Isabella described the truth about life in Hermania and that outsiders were seen as dangerous and would be chased away.

The Prince could feel his skin changing back again and quickly covered himself with his cape. Had it really been six hours of talking and laughing about each other's lives?

Isabella looked sadly upon the Prince and promised to look after him. Just as she was leaving she heard some rustling in the trees behind her. It was little Karol, the wood-carvers son. He had been watching and listening for quite a while.

Isabella wanted to know why he was up so late and made him promise to keep the Prince's location a secret.

Karol told her that some villagers were wandering the forest and he had followed them to the start of the "forbidden road". He would often roam the forest looking for bird's eggs which he collected and would have to climb trees and crawl along branches.

Then she heard more voices. Some lanterns were shining through the branches of the trees. It was a search party looking for the "beast".

When they saw Isabella and Karol they wondered what they were doing at such a late hour at night. They looked at the empty food bags and dirty clothes that Isabella had packed to take home and then at little Karol who was covered in scratches and had torn clothes.

They imagined that Isabella had been giving food and cleaning clothes for the beast . . . and that Karol was being prepared for the beast's next meal. They knew that the Royal household was wondering why their food was being stolen and that extra clothes and blankets were disappearing from the clothesline. Now they were sure!

The villagers took Karol home for some hot food and to his warm bed, but Isabella was taken back to the village square where everyone was summoned for a meeting. The King was also summoned.

Karol's father tried to reassure everyone that Isabella would not harm Karol and that she may have been under the spell of the beast when she decided to feed it. The villagers were frightened and no amount of persuasion by the King would change their minds – they had decided to throw Isabella out of Hermania and deal with the beast once and for all.

The villagers all picked up sticks, stones, farm tools and even the dreaded "magic powder" that was left in their care by their ancestors. No one knew much about it, except that it should only be used in an absolute emergency . . . such as this. Then they crept quietly towards the tree where the Prince was now sleeping after eating some food and wrapping himself up in a freshly cleaned blanket.

Four barrels of magic powder were placed at the entrance to the tree hollow and a trail of the powder was sprinkled into a path fifty feet long . . . and then lit with a rag soaked in oil. The flame had transferred from a lantern to the rag and onto the powdery trail.

It 'fizzed' and 'sparkled' and 'swooshed' as the flame ran along the trail. Blue, black and grey smoke filled the air and the noise made even the bravest villager feel that something BIG was about to happen.

KABOOM! The entire tree was blown out of the ground and the surrounding soil and rocks were smashed into tiny pieces. There was nothing left . . . but wait . . . one flower had appeared where the tree had stood. It was purple and had red spots and was in full bloom.

The villagers looked at the scene of their anger and destruction and felt ashamed. They had not seen the beast at all and yet had acted like a savage angry mob. They looked at poor Isabella who was crying.

They looked at little Karol who again had followed the villagers into the forest. One of the villagers asked Karol if he had seen the beast on that previous night. After much thinking and seeing Isabella so upset with grief, he told them that the beast was all in their imaginations . . . and had never existed.

Everyone left the scene and Karol smiled back at poor Isabella who wanted to remain. Now I am not going to tell you that the beast had NOT been destroyed, for it surely had, but there is more to this tale than that.

Isabella placed a small golden fence around the flower. She did not want to wear her silly crown anymore anyway. Then she poured some water around the flower and turned to go home.

Many weeks passed by and things were returning to normal. Isabella would visit the flower every day and pour water around it. Sometimes she would bring his book and read from it and have a quiet laugh about how wrong it was to judge others by their appearance or from what other people may think about them.

On one particular visit she was very tired and sadly decided to place the book next to the flower. Reaching over, her tears mingled with the soil and some made their way into the book, smudging the words and pictures. The gold crown suddenly started to shake and all the ink in the book drained out leaving blank pages. The flower tilted over as if it was going to die.

Then suddenly the very earth began to shake and . . . rising from the ground before her teary eyes, the Prince began to emerge. His head fitted through the crown and his body rose vertically up before he fell sideways onto the ground. Strangely, the crown was now around his neck, not able to be removed.

Isabella was stunned and reached out for her crown to touch it. The Prince took her hand softly and told her he had been saved from the curse by her tears of love and commitment. He had no idea why the crown was around his neck or who would have thought up such an unusual situation.

They talked and laughed and after a short while, they walked into the village square amid most strange looks from the villagers, for they recognised the crown as Isabella's. Now this was a tough gig for anyone to follow but Isabella was no slouch when it came to getting what she wanted or getting out of trouble. They all started asking questions at the same time, such as who was he, where was he from and why was her thick gold crown stuck around his neck.

Isabella looked at the Prince and told him to wave at the villagers, which he did, with a wide smile. Then she placed some string in his right hand and threw the attached kite into the air. As the kite drifted upwards, the villagers were amazed and started clapping and nodding. Then they all looked back at the crown, too small to get over his head. Well maybe it is a small item to overlook when a kite is flying overhead.

Isabella shouted out to the gathered crowd.

> "This is my own Prince from the Sand People. I have captured him and he has captured my heart. I have used my crown to show others that nothing is impossible. No one can ever remove it. It is in a safe place for when I become Queen one day. Over time, we will get to know the Sand People and their ways . . . and they our ways. My Prince will teach you all how to read and write so that you can pass on your stories and customs to future generations and to those outside our kingdom."

The Prince thought that was a 'pain-in-the-neck', although he supposed that it may have been the crown. The villagers all learnt how to read and write and would often send funny notes down the mountain to the Sand People by kite.

Unfortunately, the Sand People were very afraid and quickly burnt every kite. Maybe it is because I told them that kites turn into blood-sucking bats.

Who knows what other silly things they fear?

Roxy Dog

Livie phoned me up and said today that she didn't want to go out – or to play

Well I tried to understand - when she said

"Dreams only come true, if you stay in bed"

Then she drew a "C" on a rock, see.

And believed that the rock would unlock, see.

Rock - C - Rock - C

Roxy! Roxy Dog!

So I went to see her older sister

To tell her to get up, we really missed her.

She said "I dreamt about a dog that needs release"

And made a "C" with her hand, did our Elisse.

Yes they drew a "C" on a rock, see.

And believed that the rock would unlock, see.

Rock - C - Rock - C

Roxy! Roxy Dog!

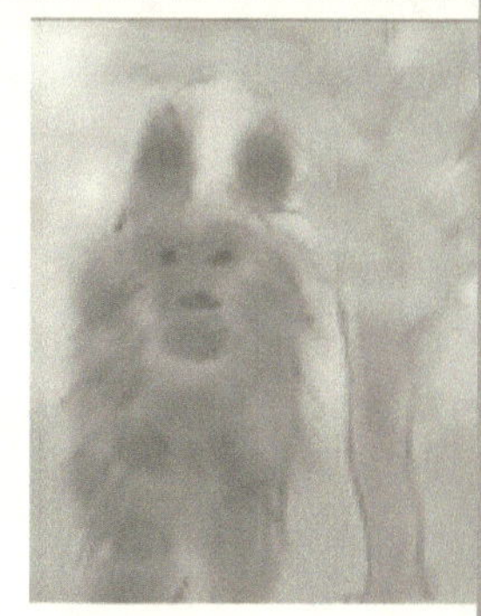

Now the next time when I saw them,

there were three, see.

Livie and Elisse and a dog, see.

I said "Is that the dog you dreamed in bed that must now be walked each day and fed?"

Then they both pointed where their dream rock used to be.

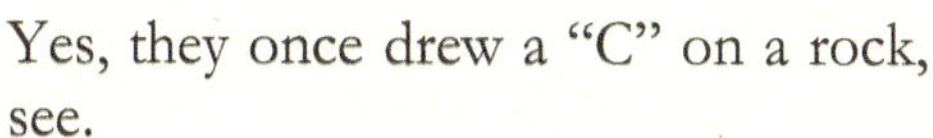

Yes, they once drew a "C" on a rock, see.

And dreamed that the rock would unlock, see.

Rock - C - Rock - C

Roxy! Roxy Dog!

Roxy! Roxy Dog!

Note: This is a song.

Windswept

Windswept, dark-grey, cold sombre moods.

Towel-draped, so sad and blue.

Silent movements. Deep-sighing.

Cute!

Remembering now, life's simple rule . . .

"Why, when summer ends . . . it's time for school".

About the Author:

Stefan Nicholson, MA (Swinburne) has had a multiple career in science and technology with an unstoppable undercurrent to author books and compose music.

He is the author of fourteen books which include novels, short stories, poetry and an invented international symbol language called "Symbolic Art Notation".

Born in England with a Polish father before migrating to Tasmania, Stefan now lives in Hobart, Tasmania on his boat "Nickinoff" in the Prince of Wales Bay Marina.

Latest books:

'Symbolic Art Notation' – a complete language using pictures

'Jemma short stories' – for ages 10 plus

'Circle in a Spiral' – sci-fi thriller for high school plus

'Short Comedy Routines for Novices'

'Shadows, Anxiety & Narrative' - 62 poems

Ruby Trilogy (adolescent fiction):

1 - **"Spy within a Ruby"**

2 - **"Diamond for a Ruby"**

3 - **"Ruby's Covert Mission"** – coming 2019

and an original music CD – 'Pictures of Life'

www.ingramcontent.com/pod-product-compliance
Lightning Source LLC
LaVergne TN
LVHW051023080826
845145LV00009B/2776

* 9 7 8 0 6 4 8 2 9 5 3 9 6 *